## Usi

When goir
with your child, y.
the story first, talking about it
and discussing the pictures,
or start with the sounds pages
at the beginning.

If you start at the front of the book,
read the words and point to the pictures.
Emphasise the **sound** of the letter.

Encourage your child to think
of the other words beginning with
and including the same sound.
The story gives you the opportunity
to point out these sounds.

After the story, slowly go through the
sounds pages at the end.

Always praise and encourage
as you go along. Keep your
reading sessions short and stop
if your child loses interest.

Throughout the series, the order in which the sounds
are introduced has been carefully planned to
help the important link between reading and writing.
This link has proved to be a powerful boost to
the development of both skills.

SOUNDS FEATURED IN THIS BOOK
v   w   wh   wr

The sounds introduced are repeated
and given emphasis in the practice books,
where the link between reading and writing is at the
root of the activities and games.

Ladybird books are widely available, but in case of
difficulty may be ordered by post or telephone from:

Ladybird Books – Cash Sales Department
Littlegate Road  Paignton  Devon TQ3 3BE
Telephone 0803 554761

A catalogue record for this book is available
from the British Library

Published by Ladybird Books Ltd  Loughborough  Leicestershire  UK
Ladybird Books Inc  Auburn  Maine 04210  USA

# Ladybird

## Say the Sounds
# Flying saucer

by JILL CORBY

illustrated by PETER WILKS

# Vv

Vaz

van

very

voice

every

vase

heaven

ever

never

over

oven

vanish

veil

leaves

5

# Ww

watch

when

where

win

way

Wex

walk

water

wish

word

wind

well

Wednesday

wave

week

wall

Jenny and Ben were riding their bikes. Jenny was riding down the hill on her bike and Ben was riding up the hill.

They were riding their bikes up
and down the hills.

Then Ben saw something.
Something very strange.
It came up over the hill.
"Look, Jenny, look up there.
What is that?" he asked her.

"I don't know. I don't know what it is," she said to him. It was coming down to the hill now. They put their bikes by the tree and looked at it.

It came down by them. They
looked at the strange thing.

"What are we going to do?"
Jenny asked.

"Where do you think it has come from?" Ben asked her.

Then two strange creatures came out of it...

The first creature came out of it quickly. He was green all over.

Ben and Jenny looked at him.

Then the next creature came out of it. She was red all over. They looked at her.

"Don't they look strange?" Jenny said.

The first one came up to Ben
and said, "My name is Vaz."
Then the next one came up to
Jenny and said, "My name is
Wex."

Jenny and Ben told them their
names. They all looked at the
bikes by the tree.
Vaz asked, "What are they?
What do they do?"

Ben and Jenny got on their
bikes and rode up and down
the hills.
Then Vaz got on Ben's bike.
They told him what to do.
But he fell off.

Next Wex got on Jenny's bike.
They told her what to do.
But she fell off, too.

Then Ben held the
bike for Vaz.
But he fell off
once more.

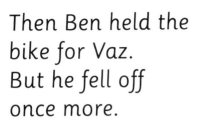

Jenny held her
bike for Wex.
But she fell off
once more.

So then Ben rode his bike with
Vaz on the back.
And Jenny rode her bike with
Wex on the back.

They were all very pleased.

Then Vaz told Jenny that they
were very hungry.
"And I'm hungry, too," Ben said.
"We are all hungry so let's go
home," Jenny told them.

So Ben and Jenny rode home
on their bikes with Vaz and
Wex on the back.

Then they saw some cars. The cars were going very fast.
Vaz and Wex were scared of the fast cars.

First Vaz made Ben's bike go up
over the cars.
Then Wex made Jenny's bike go
up over the cars, too.
At first Jenny and Ben were
scared.

Some dogs saw them and barked. Vaz and Wex were scared once more.

The dogs barked and barked.

Then Jenny and Wex
disappeared.

They disappeared so quickly that
the dogs were very surprised.

Then they all came back and were riding their bikes once more.

It got dark. Ben and Jenny walked their bikes home.

Vaz and Wex walked home with them.

They were surprised by the lights.

"What do you need lights for?" Wex asked Jenny.

"We don't need lights like that," Vaz told her.

Jenny told Vaz that when it was dark they could not see. "We need lights so that we can see where to go," she told him.

Wex said that they could make their own light.

"Look, we make our own light in the dark. Like this," Vaz told them.

Jenny and Ben were surprised that Vaz and Wex could make their own light.

When they got home, Jenny and Ben could not see their dad. So they walked into their house and Vaz and Wex walked into the house, too.

First Jenny gave Wex some
biscuits. Then she gave Vaz
some, too.
Ben gave Vaz a drink. Then he
gave Wex a drink.
Vaz and Wex were very pleased.

Then Dad came home. He walked
into the house and saw Ben
and Jenny with their drinks.
Wex held the plate of biscuits.
Dad could not see Wex and Vaz.

They had disappeared. He could
see a plate with two biscuits on
it. But when he looked once
more, the plate had gone.
Dad was surprised. There
was something strange here.
He could not make it out.

When Dad had gone, Vaz and
Wex came back once more.
"We must go now," Wex told
Ben and Jenny.
"We must go home, quickly."

"Goodbye, goodbye," they said.
"Goodbye, goodbye," said
Jenny and Ben.
Then Vaz and Wex had gone.

# Vv

Which of these has the V sound in its name?

# Ww

Read and listen.

weather   work

water   win   well   wood

walk   would   we   away

swim   sway   flew   few

dew   cow   how   now

# wh

sound **W**

when

what

why

whale

sound **h** who whose

whole

# wr

wring

wrote

wrong

sound **r**

writing

## New words used in the story

**Words introduced  49**

# Learn to read with Ladybird

## Read with me

A scheme of 16 graded books which uses a look-say approach to introduce beginner readers to the first 300 most frequently used words in the English language (Key Words). Children learn whole words and, with practice and repetition, build up a reading vocabulary.

*Support material:* Pre-reader, Practice and Play Books, Book and Cassette Packs, Picture Dictionary, Picture Word Cards

## Say the Sounds

A phonically based, graded reading scheme of 8 titles. It teaches children the sounds of individual letters and letter combinations, enabling them to feel confident in approaching Key Words.

*Support material:*
Practice Books, Double Cassette Pack, Flash Cards

## Read it yourself

A graded series of 24 books to help children to learn new words in the context of a familiar story. These readers follow on from the pre-reading series, **Read together**, and can be used in conjunction with any Ladybird reading scheme.